Dear mouse friends,
Welcome to the world of

Geronimo Stilton

THE RODENT'S GAZETTE
EDITORIAL STAFF

Geronimo Stilton
A learned and brainy
mouse; editor of
The Rodent's Gazette

Thea Stilton
Geronimo's sister and
special correspondent at
The Rodent's Gazette

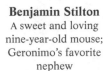

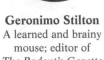

Trap Stilton
An awful joker;
Geronimo's cousin and
owner of the store
Cheap Junk for Less

Benjamin Stilton
A sweet and loving
nine-year-old mouse;
Geronimo's favorite
nephew

Geronimo Stilton

GET INTO GEAR, STILTON!

Scholastic Inc.

No part of this publication may be reproduced, stored in a retrieval system, or transmitted in any form or by any means, electronic, mechanical, photocopying, recording, or otherwise, without written permission from the copyright holder. For information regarding permission, please contact: Atlantyca S.p.A., Via Leopardi 8, 20123 Milan, Italy; e-mail foreignrights@atlantyca.it, www.atlantyca.com.

ISBN 978-0-545-48194-6

Published by Scholastic Inc., 557 Broadway, New York, NY 10012.
SCHOLASTIC and associated logos are trademarks and/or registered trademarks of Scholastic Inc.

Text by Geronimo Stilton
Original title *Ingrana la marcia, Stilton!*
Cover by Giuseppe Ferrario (design) and Giulia Zaffaroni (color)
Illustrations by Alessandro Muscillo (design) and
Christian Aliprandi (color)
Graphics by Chiara Cebraro

Special thanks to AnnMarie Anderson
Translated by Lidia Morson Tramontozzi
Interior design by Kay Petronio

12 11 10 9 8 7 6 5 4 3 2 1   13 14 15 16 17 18/0

Printed in the U.S.A.   40
First printing, July 2013

Thirty stories below New Mouse City in an undisclosed location, a very sophisticated robotic vehicle called Solar is stored in a secret laboratory. Solar is the only robot of its kind in the entire world. It can see, hear, and even talk! Solar will only allow one mouse to be its driver — the one and only Geronimo Stilton! Too bad Geronimo can barely drive and his driver's license has expired. Holey cheese! What's a gentlemouse to do? Turn the page to read the absolutely true story of Geronimo and Solar's first encounter and their top-secret mission.

·SOLAR·

A Cheerful Spring Morning

It was a cheerful Spring morning in New Mouse City. The birds were singing, the air smelled fresh and clean, and it seemed as if everyone was smiling at me. I left my house whistling and headed toward my office at 17 Swiss Cheese Center.

Oh, I'm sorry! I forgot to introduce myself. My name is Stilton, *Geronimo Stilton*. I'm the editor of *The Rodent's Gazette*, the most famous newspaper on Mouse Island.

On my way to work, I stopped at the newsstand and bought a copy of my favorite MAGAZINE, *The Collector of Cheeses*. Then I saw the **NEWSPAPER** headlines: Someone had **STOLEN** Duchess Catherine Rodenton's seventy-three-carat **diamond** necklace! Holey cheese!

I headed to my favorite **coffee shop** for breakfast. The owner, Flip Hotpaws,

Thank you!

Yum!

served me my usual order of a cappuccino and a delicious **CHEESE-FILLED** pastry. After my breakfast, I passed the bookstore in Singing Stone Square and glanced in the window.

I was happy to see that the bookstore was featuring one of my bestselling books in the front window. An older rodent recognized me and asked for my *autograph*.

I'm a very shy mouse, and I flushed with **embarrassment**.

"What will your next book be about, Mr. Stilton?" she asked.

"I haven't decided yet," I told her.

After I signed her **BOOK**, I continued to my office.

I walked **SLOWLY** along the sidewalk, deep in thought. Who had **stolen** the **ENORMOUSE** diamond necklace? And what should my next book be about? Maybe I would write a **comedy** or a LOVE STORY. Or I could write a **mystery** about a jewel thief! With my head in the

For the love of bananas, watch out!

CLOUDS, I stepped off the curb to cross the street.

Suddenly, there was the **sound** of SCREECHING brakes. I spun quickly and saw that something **LARGE** and YELLOW was about to hit me.

I tried to jump out of the way, but it was too late. I flew up, up, up into the air and came **SMASHING** down to the ground in the middle of the street!

How Are You, Stilton?

I looked up and saw the faces of five rodents PEERING down at me. I recognized the newsstand owner, **FLIP HOTPAWS**, and the older rodent from the bookstore. Everyone was **SHOUTING**.

"How are you feeling, Mr. Stilton?"

Oh, my!

Poor thing!

What a fall!

Ouchie!

In the midst of all those voices, I thought I heard a **FAMILIAR** one. Where had I heard that before? Who could it be?

"How are you, my dear Stilton?" the voice SQUEAKED.

"Ahem, I think I'm still **alive** . . . or am I?" I replied.

I heard the wail of the ambulance *siren* growing louder and louder, and then I *fainted*.

When I came to, I saw nothing but WHITE, WHITE, WHITE. For a second, I was afraid I had died. Then I felt a huge **pain** in my tail, and I knew I was still alive!

I was in a **hospital** surrounded by the rodents who had come to my aid. They all watched as the doctor wrapped my tail in a **bandage**.

"**Ouchie, ouchie, ouchie!**" I whimpered. "What happened?"

"You **broke** your tail, Mr. Stilton," said a doctor. "You had an accident."

"A-an **accident**?" I stammered. "Oh, yes, the **diamond** — I mean, the **newspaper** — that is, the autograph. What I meant to say is I remember now. I was about to cross the street when —"

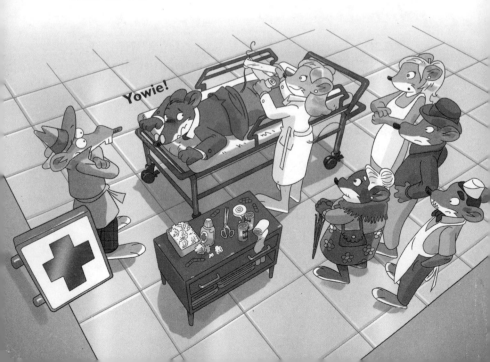

Yowie!

Suddenly, I remembered everything.

"I was **HIT** by a car!" I shouted. "Who would do such a thing?"

"It was me, Stilton . . ." a familiar voice **SQUEAKED**.

I turned and saw my childhood friend **Hercule Poirat**.

"You did it?!" I exclaimed. "Why? Why, oh, why did you hit me?"

Hercule looked ashamed.

"Sorry, Stilton!" he apologized. "I tried to **stop**, but it was too *late*. I had a green light, and you were in the middle of the street."

"You weren't paying **attention**, Mr. Stilton," the newsstand owner scolded me.

"That's right," Flip Hotpaws agreed. "You were **VEEEERY** distracted!"

An Enormouse Banana Peel

The emergency room door **flew** open, and my whole family **BURST** in. Everyone was shouting at the same time.

"Geronimo, you're **ALIVE!**"

"You could have been **killed**. . . ."

"You just made it by a **whisker**. . . ."

The doctor finished **BANDAGING** my tail, and I was released from the hospital. But my family members wouldn't stop **scolding** me.

It's all your fault!

Pay more attention!

"It's all your **fault**!" Grandfather William Shortpaws barked.

"You have to pay more **attention**,

dearest nephew," Aunt Sweetfur told me with a look of concern.

"You're constantly **DISTRACTED**, Geronimo!" my sister, Thea, chided.

"Where was your head?" my cousin Trap asked me. "It must have been in the **clouds**, like always."

"What were you thinking, Uncle?" my nephew Benjamin asked SWEETLY.

"Let me tell you what happened," Hercule said.

You're constantly distracted!

Where was your head?

What were you thinking?

Let me tell you what happened.

"I was driving the Bananamobile — you've seen it before, haven't you?" Hercule asked. "It's an enormouse yellow car shaped like a banana. It's pretty hard to miss. Anyway, the light was green, but suddenly Geronimo was in front of me! Luckily, I was going slowly. He wasn't paying any attention! His head was in the CLOUDS for sure. . . ."

Everyone shook their heads and muttered in agreement.

I was really offended. I hadn't been distracted on purpose! I was just thinking about the diamond necklace that had been stolen and concentrating on ideas for my next book. When had DAYDREAMING become a crime?

To get away from all the finger-pointing and to have some peace, I decided to retreat to my office.

"I'm coming with you, Geronimo," Grandfather William **ANNOUNCED**. "I want to keep an **EYE** on you!"

He followed me all the way to the offices of *The Rodent's Gazette*. As soon as we got there, one of the staff writers, **Priscilla Prettywhiskers**, walked up to me and WHiSPeReD something in my ear.

"There's someone **IMPORTANT** waiting for you in your office," she said. Then she lowered her voice even more. "It's the *mayor* — fur, whiskers, and all!"

"Double twisted rat tails!" I exclaimed. "What an **honor**!"

I entered my office, and Mayor Frederick Fuzzypaws greeted me **cordially**.

"Good morning, Mr. Stilton!" he said. "Oh, and good morning, Mr. Shortpaws! I have **great** news for both of you. The city will be choosing a publishing company for a very prestigious new safety awareness campaign, and we thought of you," he explained.

Grandfather began to **twirl** his whiskers proudly.

"That sounds mouserific," he said. "What's it about?"

"The city is preparing a *booklet* on road safety education that will be distributed to all the schools in New Mouse City," the mayor replied.

Good morning!

"You have no idea how many mice don't know how to **safely** get around the **STREETS** of New Mouse City," the mayor explained.

"Oh, I know one of those mice myself!" Grandfather said as he shot me a knowing glare.

I turned as red as a tomato.

"Er, yes, well, we received a lot of offers from COMPETING publishing companies," the mayor continued. "For example, Sally Ratmousen's company, *The Daily Rat*, made a fine offer. But we want *The Rodent's Gazette* to do this booklet!"

At the mere **MENTION** of *The Daily Rat* and Sally Ratmousen, my

SALLY RATMOUSEN

She is the unscrupulous editor of **The Daily Rat.** Her motto is: If there is no news, we'll invent it!

grandfather turned **PURPLE**. She and her newspaper are our biggest **rivals**.

"I'm glad you came to us," Grandfather said quickly. "We'll make a booklet that's **whisker-licking** good. We know how to handle road safety, right, Geronimo?"

"Of course!" I agreed *quickly*.

Suddenly, the mayor happened to notice my **BANDAGED** tail.

"Mr. Stilton, what happened?" he asked.

"Oh, **NOTHING**," I replied hastily.

"What do you mean 'nothing'?" the mayor insisted. "It's all *wrapped* up! Did you have an accident?"

My grandfather jumped in.

"You see, my grandson . . . er . . . he slipped on a banana peel!" he said. "Yes, it was an **ENORMOUSE** banana peel."

I opened my eyes wide in **surprise**.

"Huh? What peel?" I asked. "What **banana**?"

Grandfather elbowed me in the side — hard.

"Ouch!" I squeaked.

"It was an enormousely **HUGE PEEL!**" Grandfather repeated. "Right, grandson?"

"Yes, yes. It was **huge!**" I agreed quickly as I rubbed my side. "It was a banana peel as big as . . . a **car!**"

"Ah, good, good," the mayor replied, looking **relieved**. "For a second, I thought you didn't know how to travel the **STREETS** safely! In about a week, your company will officially present the booklet in New Mouse City's main square. Every reporter and television crew on **Mouse Island** will be there! And Mr. Stilton, you will give a live demonstration on **safe DRiViNG**!"

"Who, me?" I asked nervously. "I have to drive in front of **EVERYONE**?"

"Why, yes," the mayor replied. "Is there a **problem**? You have a license, right? You know how to *drive safely* through the streets of New Mouse City, correct?"

He **STARED** at me, and my grandfather **STARED** at me, and I had a **very, very, veeeeery** bad feeling. But what could I do?

Hmm...

"Of course I have a driver's license," I said **confidently**.

20

"I've had it since I was **sixteen**!"

"Good, good," the mayor said with a smile. "And it's valid, right? The license hasn't EXPIRED, has it?

He peered at me, a *serious* look on his face as he waited for my answer.

I stood there with a smile **frozen** on my face as I frantically checked the license. *Squeak!* It EXPIRED years ago! I never drive, so I forgot to renew it!

My grandfather looked at me with RAISED eyebrows.

"Is there a **PROBLEM**, Grandson?" he asked.

I turned as PALE as a slice of mozzarella.

"No—no," I stammered. "Everything's just fine!"

But everything wasn't fine! I had a big problem on my paws.

CONGRATULATIONS! IT'S A NEW RECORD!

The **mayor** got up to leave.

"Perfect!" he said, an **ENORMOUSE** smile on his face. "Mr. Stilton, I'll see you in a week at the **ceremony**. And don't forget to bring the license!"

"Of course, of course," I stuttered. "The **LICENSE**. Yes, of course!"

I was **sweating**, and I felt sick to my stomach. I was overcome by total **PANIC**. My license had **EXPIRED**! I wouldn't be able to drive during the ceremony!

WHAT A MESS!

I didn't dare say anything to Grandfather. Instead, I *decided* to call my friend PETUNIA PRETTY PAWS.

The truth is, I have a **huge** crush on Petunia, but I can never get up the courage to ask her out on a date! Still, I called to ask for her **help**.

"Hi, G!" Petunia answered the phone. She listened to my problem and came up with a **solution**. "You have to go to a very good **DRIVING SCHOOL**. Ask them what to do. Maybe you still have time to renew your license."

I remembered that there was a little driving school right on my street. It was called The Very Best Driving School in New Mouse City,

so I figured it had to be good!

I thanked Petunia and headed straight there.

"Good morning, how may I help you?" a kind-looking rodent asked **sweetly**.

"Well, er, I know how to **drive**, yes, I do, but it's as if I don't." I tried to explain. "I never drive, but I have a **license**, and I have to drive in a **CEREMONY** next week, and — please, oh, please, can you **help me**?"

"Come this way!" a **SHRILL** voice behind me shouted in reply.

It was the owner of the driving school, **Rusty Carr**. He was a very **well-dressed** rodent in a suit and tie the color of **cheddar**

cheese. His shiny eyes were as **black** as olives and as **piercing** as needles.

Filled with hope, I handed him my license.

License No. 13171317
Geronimo Stilton
Mouse Island

He took a **very quick** look at the license and shook his head.

"I have two pieces of news for you," he said. "**First**, this license has **expired**. And **second**, you have to **RETAKE** the driving test."

Retake the test?! I wanted to **CRY**.

"To get a **DRIVER'S LICENSE**, you need to pass both the written test and the road test," Rusty continued.

"I have to take TWO tests?" I asked. My whiskers trembled with fear. It's true that I hadn't driven in a LOOOOONG time, but I knew how to do it! I didn't have time to study for TWO tests — the ceremony was in one week!

"But I passed both the written and driving tests once," I argued. "And I'm a VERY GOOD driver, even if I don't do it often."

"Quiet, quiet, quiet!" he ordered as he gave me a sheet of paper with ten questions on it.

"No excuses. If you think you know everything already, then take this quiz and let's see how you do."

I glanced at the sheet and turned as green as a moldy piece of Brie.

I didn't know any of the answers!

I did the best I could and then handed him the **PAPER**. With a red pencil, he began **CROSSING OUT** one thing after another.

"Not one **correct answer**!" he announced. "Absolutely **none**. Congratulations, you've set a new record!"

WHAT DOES THIS MEAN?
~~Crumbling cheese may fall on your car?~~
Noooo! Danger: Falling Rocks

WHAT DOES THIS MEAN?
~~Drive in a squiggly line?~~
Noooo! Slippery when wet!

WHAT DOES THIS MEAN?
~~Treasure buried here?~~
Noooo! Railroad crossing.

WHAT DOES THIS MEAN?
~~Well, let's see. . .~~

LEFT! RIGHT! STOP!

The written test was a *DISASTER*.

"But within a week I have to drive in front of everybody!" I wailed. My whiskers were **trembling** from the stress. "The **mayor** will be there, and reporters, and TV news cameras. Oh, what am I going to do? Please help me!"

"Relax, relax," Rusty assured me. "All you have to do is take some **DRIVING** lessons, do some **studying**, and both tests will be a **BREEZE**!"

"Okay, where do I sign up?" I asked.

"First you have to fully **commit** yourself to learning how to drive," he warned.

"I'll commit myself!" I **PROMISED**.

"I'll **yell** at you if I have to, **understand**?"

Rusty asked.

"Yes, yes," I agreed, getting desperate. "**yell** at me all you want!"

"If you're sure . . ." Rusty replied hesitantly.

"I'm sure!" I squeaked.

"Then hop in," Rusty told me. "The **FIRST LESSON** is about to start!"

I buckled my **SEAT BELT**, turned on the **left** signal, checked the rearview **mirror**, and slowly began to pull away from the **CURB**.

"**WAIT!**" Rusty shouted. "You forgot to check your SIDE mirrors! We don't want to be flattened like a slice of Swiss, do we?"

I looked in both side mirrors and saw that the coast was clear, so I began to proceed **cautiously**.

The entire time, Rusty *shouted* commands at me.

"Turn **LEFT**! Now **RIGHT**! Slow down! *Accelerate*! Now **BRAAAAAAKE**! Now *Accelerate* again, then turn **RIGHT**,

What are you doing?

Hmm . . .

Aaaaaah!

Slow down!

and **RIGHT**, and **RIGHT** . . ."

My head was spinning from all his orders.

"Proceed **straight**. Now go **FORWARD**! Go **BACK**! Right! Left! **STOP!** Brake! No, not like that! Can't you see we're merging? You have to remain alert and **observant**."

I was trying my best, but it seemed like everything I did was **WRONG**!

"Hey, what's the matter with you?" Rusty asked. "That's a *crosswalk*! Pedestrians

Turn right, not left!

Heeeeeeeeelp!

Tsk . . . No, that's wrong!

Not like this!

have the **RIGHT OF WAY**, got it? What are you doing? That's a one-way street! Didn't you see the SIGN?"

He shook his head at me.

Then things got even **worse**!

"Now it's going to get more **difficult**," Rusty warned me. "You can never be DISTRACTED while driving, Mr. Stilton — it's very **DANGEROUS**! I am going to ask you questions to **distract** you, but you have to keep your concentration! You'll drive and answer me at the SAME TIME!"

MOLDY MOZZARELLA! This was not going to be good!

"So, how's work?" Rusty began. "What's your SISTER'S name? What's **THREE** times **SIX**, divided by two, plus EIGHTEEN minus **THREE**?* Answer me — go ahead, ANSWER!"

* The answer is twenty-four!

"Er, it's f-fine," I stammered. "Lea! I mean Thea! Um, thirty-two?"

"Now turn **right** and merge into traffic!" Rusty shouted. "Now **STOP**!"

I slammed on the brakes.

"Didn't you see the **STOP** sign?!" Rusty scolded me. "We were almost flattened like **pancakes**! Now keep a safe distance from that truckful of **manure**!"

I slowed down a bit, but Rusty continued to hound me.

Yuck!

"The stench may be vile, but you can't pass that truck," he continued. "There's a solid **LINE**! And don't drive too close. If the truck stops short, we might hit it, and then that stinky load of manure will land right on top of us!"

I slowed down even more.

"What's that NoiSE?" Rusty asked. "You scraped the bumper against that curb! **Yikes!** You missed hitting that post, but only by less than an *inch*! There's an **AMBULANCE** coming. Don't you hear the siren? Yield and let it pass! CONGRATULATIONS! You've broken another record: ten mistakes in less than an hour!"

He shook his head.

"As far as that official ceremony with the mayor, there are only two solutions," Rusty continued. "Either get someone else to take your place, or start getting **SERIOUS** about these driving lessons!"

HUMILIATED, I lowered my head.

"I really am trying to be serious," I mumbled. "Tell me what I have to do to IMPROVE!"

Rusty studied me intensely with his **shiny** black eyes.

"Each morning at seven o'clock on the **dot**, you must have a written lesson," he said.

I nodded in **agreement**.

"Then after that, you need to have a **Loooooong** driving lesson," he continued. "MAYBE, just maybe, you might pass the test. But I have to be truthful with you: Your situation is pretty **DESPERATE**!"

I agreed to the LESSONS. What else could I do?

MY FIRST DAY IN DRIVING SCHOOL

1. I ALMOST RAN OVER A RODENT IN THE CROSSWALK!

2. OOPS! I DIDN'T YIELD THE RIGHT OF WAY!

3. I ALMOST HIT A TRUCK FULL OF MANURE! YUCK!

4. WHILE IN REVERSE, I HIT A CONCRETE POST.

5. I HAD A TEENSY-WEENSY PROBLEM WITH PARKING.

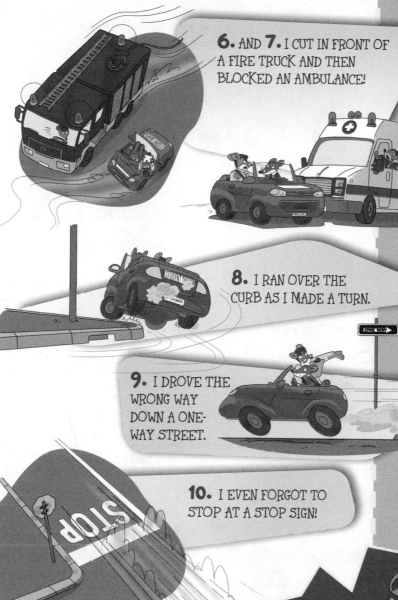

You're a Loose Cannon!

From that day on, I arrived **punctually** at seven o'clock every morning for my written lesson and my driving lesson. Then I **RACED** to my office to work on the booklet on **road safety** for the mayor's office.

On the morning of the fourth day, Rusty greeted me with a **DEVILISH** grin.

"Well, well, let's see if you're ready," he said, rubbing his paws together. Then he began pointing to an **ENORMOUSE** chart with lots of **STREET SIGNS** as he shouted out one question after another.

"What does this **SIGN** mean?" he asked. "And this one? And how about this one? **HMMMM?**"

I **froze**. I couldn't remember **anything**!

"**Bicycle path**'?" I guessed. It was the first thing that **popped** into my head. "No, no. Maybe 'no entry to **bicycles**'? Or 'switch the circles'? 'Caution, **GEOMETRY** test ahead'? Maybe, 'right of way'? Or maybe . . . I don't know!"

I was so **stressed out**, my tail was twisted into tiny knots.

I COULDN'T REMEMBER ANYTHING!

Rusty threw his paws in the air.

"I don't believe it!" he exclaimed. "You're a loose cannon! You're LUCKY your license expired, because you really needed this ReFReSHeR! You're a complete basket of nerves! But don't worry — I'll help you get through this."

After the written lesson, I took my DriViNG LeSSON, and then I went straight to the office to work on the ROAD SAFETY booklet. In the booklet, I tried to explain the importance of abiding by the rules of the road.

There were only three more days until the booklet was due, so I worked day and **night**. I finally finished it and emailed it to the editor. Then I collapsed and fell ASLEEP with my snout on top of my laptop computer.

I dreamed that an ENORMOUSE traffic

cop was **blowing** his whistle and shaking his head as he wrote me a **TRAFFIC TICKET**.

"You're not ready, Mr. Stilton," he said. "You still have to work **very** hard . . . **very, very** hard, yes, EXTREMELY hard!"

A Golden Cloud

When I woke up the following morning at ten minutes to seven, the imprints of all the computer keys were stamped on my face.

I rushed over to The Very Best Driving School in New Mouse City for my fifth day of lessons. Everything was going very well, and Rusty even let a teeny tiny compliment escape.

"Not bad, not bad," he said. "You're ALMOST ready!"

But that's when something strange happened.

I heard a police siren behind me and I instinctively pulled over to the side of the road. It was a good thing I did because an instant later, a golden car whizzed by

me. It was moving so *fast* I thought it was a **missile**!

The car's motor made no noise. It only emitted a strange **HUM**, like a purring cat. I tried to figure out who was driving the **MYSTERIOUS** vehicle, but the windows were **TINTED** and I couldn't see inside. But I did see a strange symbol of a **golden sun** on the car's hood.

Immediately after the car drove by, a **SILVER** car that was otherwise identical to the gold one went **ZOOMING** by. It was almost as though the silver car was **chasing** the golden one!

"Huh?" Rusty asked. "Wha —?"

Whatever he said was **DROWNED OUT** by the sound of the police sirens as they chased after **BOTH** cars.

Then something incredibly **STRANGE** happened. The **golden** car stopped right in front of us. The sun's rays **illuminated** it like a golden star and I peered into the driver's side, trying to get a glimpse of the **DRIVER**.

Suddenly, we heard a loud **CLICK** and the golden car

Click!

DISAPPEARED!

The SILVER car that was following the golden car accelerated. A few seconds later, it slipped over the HORIZON and was out of sight.

The police car pulled up alongside us, and INSpector Clue Rat climbed out. He is New Mouse City's CHIEF OF POLICE.

"Cheddar cheese sticks!" Inspector Rat exclaimed in frustration. "Those two cars got away!"

He turned and saw Rusty and me.

"Mr. Stilton!" he said. "Did you see that? What do you think made that golden car DISAPPEAR?"

I shook my head.

"I have no idea," I replied. "It was very MYSTERIOUS. But I did hear a clicking sound, which makes me think there was some sort of **mechanical** trick."

I turned to ask Rusty his opinion, but he was calling someone on his cell phone (**who?**), whispering something (**what?**), and looking mysterious (**why?**).

A second later, he hung up the phone.

"Lesson's over," Rusty said to me **impatiently**. "Let's **GOOOOO**, Mr. Stilton! I have a very **IMPORTANT** meeting to attend."

Psst . . . pssst . . .

You Can
Call Me Sol

We drove back to **The Very Best Driving School in New Mouse City** in silence, which was very UNUSUAL. Rusty usually spent every minute of my lesson **shouting** orders at me! I didn't know why he was acting so STRANGELY.

"I'll see you **TOMORROW**, Rusty!" I said as I hopped out of the car.

"No, no lessons **TOMORROW**," he replied. "I'm busy tomorrow!"

Strange! How very **STRANGE**!

I hurried to the office and worked all day to **get ready** for the big event with the mayor and to look over the final draft of the **ROAD SAFETY EDUCATION**

booklet before it was printed.

On my way home that evening, I mulled over the morning's very **STRANGE** events. Why had the silver car been chasing the gold one? And what was Rusty being so **SECRETIVE** about? I was almost at my front door when I heard a peculiar noise: **CLICK!**

Startled, I turned around and let out a yelp. A **dazzling** cloud of light appeared, and suddenly the mysterious golden car was sitting right in front of me!

As soon as it appeared, the golden car **ZOOMED** off. The same SILVER car from earlier that morning was chasing it again! I don't know why, but I had a feeling the **golden** car was in trouble. I had to **HELP** it! Without thinking,

I hailed a taxi and dashed off in **HOT PURSUIT**.

Fortunately, it was already **evening**, and there was no one on the streets of New Mouse City, so it wasn't so difficult for a **taxi** to follow the two cars.

Suddenly, I heard a sound. *Click!* The **golden** car disappeared into the night.

"Aaaah!" the taxi driver yelled. "A **GHOST** car!"

He wanted to drop me off right then and

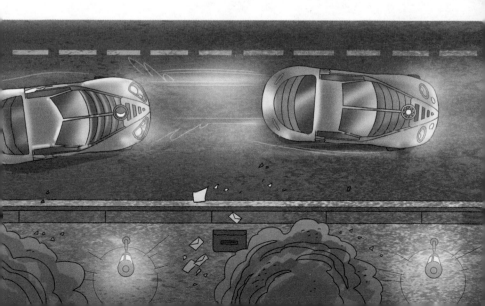

there, but I promised I'd pay him **double** if he kept on **DRIVING**. So we kept following the SILVER car. It was heading toward the **PARK**.

We followed the car, turning onto the wide, **TREE-LINED** avenue inside the park. Then I heard a familiar sound. *Click!* The mysterious golden car **rematerialized** right in front of us, and the SILVER car was right on its tail!

This time, I made up my mind not to **LOSE** them.

"Please keep up!" I told the taxi driver. "I'll pay you **TRIPLE!**"

We were right behind the silver car when I noticed that while there was a DRIVER in the silver car, there was **NO ONE** at the wheel of the **golden** car!

How was that possible?!

Suddenly I knew how I could stop the WILD car chase. I noticed that the tree-lined avenue became **wider** down the road.

"*Quick!*" I shouted to the driver. "Pass that car!"

The taxi driver **passed** the silver car and then swiftly applied the brakes. To avoid **HITTING** us, the silver car was forced to veer right onto a side street. The **golden** car took the opportunity to turn left down a different street.

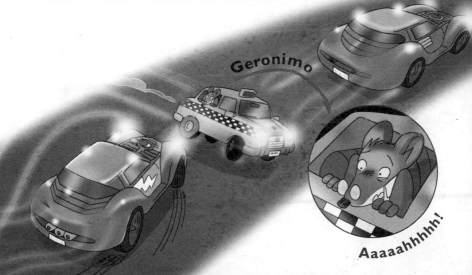

Geronimo

Aaaaahhhh!

The silver car abandoned the chase and quickly DISAPPEARED into the night, while the **TERRIFIED** cab driver stopped abruptly.

"That's it!" he squeaked. "I've had enough of GHOST cars!"

The driver **KICKED** me out of the taxi.

"I'll send your bill to you at home, Mr. Stilton!" he shouted at me as he *sped* away. "And I'm warning you: It will be very, very **EXPENSIVE**!"

Sigh . . .

He left me there all alone, feeling like a fool. I had stopped a **DANGEROUS** car chase, which was a good thing. But I couldn't figure out what had actually happened. It was a real mystery!

Then I heard a click and a **METALLIC** voice behind me. It said only two words: "*THANK YOU.*"

For a second, I thought the voice sounded a lot like my sister, Thea, but then I remembered that

Gulp!

she was away on a research trip this week, so it couldn't be her. I **JUMPED** back and **whirled** around.

"Who said that?" I **squeaked**.

Behind me was the **golden** car.

Had the car **spoken** to me? And where had it come from? Was it possible I was **dreaming**? To be absolutely certain I was awake, I pulled one of my **WHiSKeRS**.

"Yeow!" I yelped. I was definitely **awake**.

Then the voice spoke again.

"*I AM SOLAR, A ROBOT CAR,*" the voice said. "*YOU CAN CALL ME SOL. WHO ARE YOU?*"

For a second, my mouth dropped open in **amazement**. Not only did the car talk, but it also had a name: **Solar**. The name suited it perfectly, because it shone just like the **golden sun**!

As soon as I got my **WITS** about me I answered.

"Ahem, my name is Stilton, *Geronimo Stilton*."

"THANK YOU FOR HELPING ME, GERONIMO STILTON," Sol said. "I TRUST YOU. I WOULD BE HONORED IF YOU WOULD BE MY DRIVER."

I was very con·fused. Surely Sol didn't need a driver — the car was able to *drive* itself! But I was **flattered** that the car had asked me, and I didn't want to say **NO**.

"Ahem, I suppose I could, sure, yes, of course!" I stammered. "But I have a little PROBLEM: I didn't renew my **Driver's License!**"

SOL'S SECRET

"*GET IN!*" Sol ordered. "*I WILL DRIVE! FOR NOW, YOU ARE A PASSENGER! YOU'LL BE MY DRIVER AFTER YOU RENEW YOUR LICENSE. I WILL TAKE YOU TO A SECRET PLACE, A PLACE I CALL HOME.*"

So I got in the car. What **else** could I do? Sol drove for a **long time**. The motor **hummed** sweetly as the miles wore

on. It was so *quiet*, I fell asleep in the backseat as the car steered and performed all the necessary *maneuvers* to drive. I **WOKE UP** when the car stopped.

We were in a place I can't tell you about, on a **street** I can't tell you about, in front of a GOVERNMENT BUILDING I can't tell you about! That's because I gave my **RODENT'S WORD** to keep it a **SECRET**, and I **always** keep my word!

I can only tell you that Sol drove into a long, narrow RECTANGULAR room that slowly began to **descend.** I quickly realized it was an **ENORMOUSE** elevator, big enough for a **car**! The elevator stopped, the doors in front of us opened, and we found ourselves in an **immense** room where lots of **technicians** in white lab coats were busy operating some **BiZARRE** machinery.

It was a **mysterious** scientific laboratory! I was puzzled about the kinds of **experiments** that were being conducted there. I was about to ask **Sol**, but I realized the car was no longer by my side!

Sol had driven over to a mouse in a lab coat who was bent over a table **LITTERED** with different-sized test tubes filled with **colored** liquids. The scientist seemed to be completely **absorbed** in his task.

"*DAD!*" Sol exclaimed.

"**Sol!**" the scientist replied as he turned around.

As soon as the mouse turned, I recognized **PROFESSOR PAWS VON VOLT!**

"What are you doing here, professor?" I exclaimed in **surprise**.

He had a **mysterious** look about him.

"My friend, I'm so happy to see you!" he replied. "I see you've discovered my latest INVENTION: Solar, the first talking robot car in the world! It is an extremely precious experimental *prototype*. Thank you for bringing it back to me in one **PIECE**!"

"*I WOULD HAVE FIGURED IT OUT BY MYSELF*," Sol said. "*BUT HE WAS ALL RIGHT. HE IS VERY POLITE. I LIKE THIS MOUSE.*"

Professor von Volt gave **Solar** an affectionate pat.

Dad!

Sol!

"Solar is part of a **SECRET** project in the fight against **CRIME** in New Mouse City!" the professor told me. "The best scientists in all of Mouse Island worked together to build Solar," he continued. "In fact, they're all members of the **VON VOLT FAMILY**." Then he pressed a **RED** button and spoke into a microphone that came out of a little door. "Urgent meeting in **Lab Two!**"

Two **breathless** rodents arrived at once. One had red hair and **GLASSES** perched on the tip of his snout. The letter *D* was monogrammed on his shirt.

"This is my nephew, Dewey von Volt," the professor introduced him.

The other was a rodent with shiny eyes that were as **BLACK** as olives and as *piercing* as needles. It was Rusty Carr!

"Rusty?" I asked in **shock**. "What are you doing here?"

"Geronimo, do you already know my cousin Rusty?" Professor von Volt asked in **surprise**. "He's a very *skillful* mechanical engineer as well as an excellent **DRIVING** instructor!"

The next to arrive was a rodent with **RED** hair and eyes as green as *emeralds*. It was **MARGO BITMOUSE**, a well-known

Hi, there!

Here's the entire team!

computer expert in New Mouse City. She was Professor von Volt's second cousin!

Finally, a little **ROBOT** joined the group.

"And this is **Rob-8**," Professor von Volt said as he finished the introductions.

"Good! *Everyone's here!*" Professor von Volt said seriously. "Now we can give **Sol** a complete exam to make sure it hasn't been damaged. Geronimo, if you'd like, I'll have someone take you home."

But Sol **piped up**.

"*NO*," the car said. "*HE STAYS HERE. I WANT HIM TO BE MY DRIVER.*"

"Him?!" Rusty Carr shouted loudly in **protest**. "But he's a **terrible** driver! I should know — I'm his **DRIVING INSTRUCTOR**!"

I Want Him!

But Sol insisted.

"*I WANT GERONIMO STILTON,*" the car said stubbornly. "*HIM AND ONLY HIM.*"

I turned to Sol.

"Rusty is right," I admitted. "I really **stink** at driving. And I still have to **pass** the driving test!"

"*I WANT STILTON,*" the car insisted. "*STILTON, AND NO ONE ELSE!*"

Holey cheese! This car was so stubborn! Sol reminded me more and more of my sister, Thea.

Professor von Volt sighed.

"All right," he agreed reluctantly. "But first Geronimo has to read Sol's *operating manual* from front to back, and then he has to pass the **DRIVING TEST**!"

Professor von Volt turned to Rusty.

"Please have Geronimo take the test tomorrow at **dawn**, before Sol leaves for its next **mission**," he said.

Sol beeped its horn happily. **Beeeep!**

Then a bunch of technicians took Sol to the maintenance department for a **checkup**. I put my snout to the **GRINDSTONE** and began going over all the rules of the road so I would be sure to pass the driving test. After that I started studying Sol's operating manual. **Holey cheese**, it was **ten feet tall**!

Professor von Volt explained that Sol was a **ROBOT** car

Holey cheese! I'll never finish. . . .

SOLAR, THE CAR OF THE FUTURE

Also known as Sol, it's the first talking robot car in the world!

- Thanks to a very powerful electromagnetic screen, it can become invisible.
- When the driver wears a special pair of sunglasses, Sol can connect directly to the driver's mind so the two can communicate without speaking!
- Sol does not pollute the environment, and its engine is completely silent!

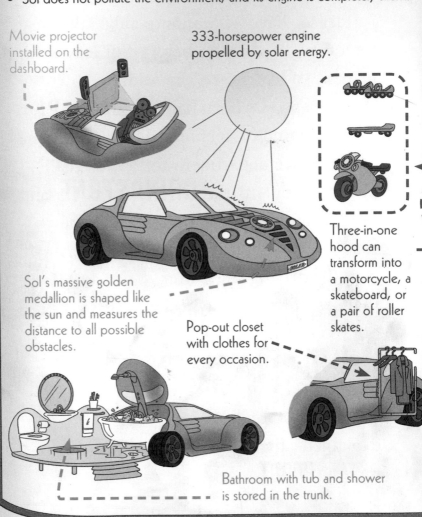

Movie projector installed on the dashboard.

333-horsepower engine propelled by solar energy.

Sol's massive golden medallion is shaped like the sun and measures the distance to all possible obstacles.

Three-in-one hood can transform into a motorcycle, a skateboard, or a pair of roller skates.

Pop-out closet with clothes for every occasion.

Bathroom with tub and shower is stored in the trunk.

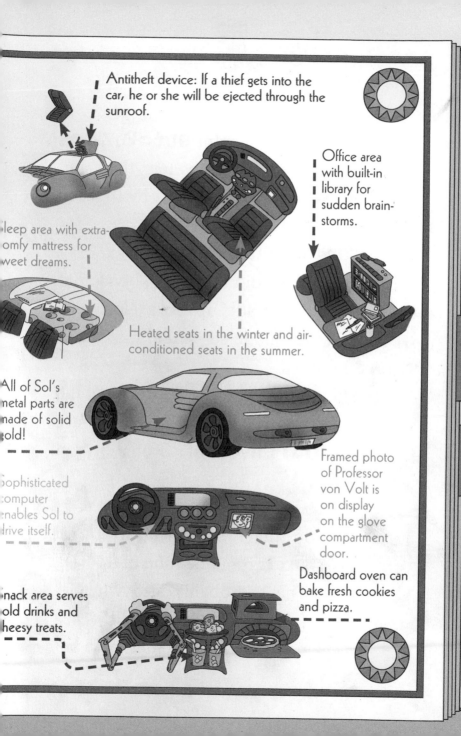

Antitheft device: If a thief gets into the car, he or she will be ejected through the sunroof.

Office area with built-in library for sudden brainstorms.

Sleep area with extra-comfy mattress for sweet dreams.

Heated seats in the winter and air-conditioned seats in the summer.

All of Sol's metal parts are made of solid gold!

Framed photo of Professor von Volt is on display on the glove compartment door.

Sophisticated computer enables Sol to drive itself.

Dashboard oven can bake fresh cookies and pizza.

Snack area serves cold drinks and cheesy treats.

with microcircuits of mini **autofuzzies**
and **bumblezizzles**, with ten thousand
cheesy watts of power provided by thirteen
different **gaggle-waggles**.

I couldn't understand a thing!

The only thing I did understand was that
the circuits that made up Sol's electronic
brain were modeled after my sister
Thea's brain!

"I tried to **RECONSTRUCT** the brain of the
smartest and toughest rodent in New Mouse
City: your **SISTER**, Thea!" Professor von
Volt told me.

Holey cheese!

So that's why whenever Sol
spoke it reminded me of **THEA**!

That's probably also why Sol
and I got *along* so well! Thea
drives me **CHEESY** sometimes, but

deep down we really do love each other.

I also found that Sol had all the **comforts** of home, including a movie projector on the dashboard and a stereo system that played relaxing **background** music that changed according to the mood of the driver. Sol could also make photocopies, send **emails**, and *MAKE* thirty-three different kinds of *hot chocolate*, including my **favorite**: with WHIPPED CREAM on top! And Sol could bake cheesy chip COOKIES and pizza, including my **favorite** variety: triple cheese!

By pushing a button, one of the backseats became a *comfy* bed with a very soft mattress and a TiNY built-in nightstand and lamp.

And the trunk transformed itself into a *POP-UP* bathroom equipped with every necessity imaginable: a tub with ENERGIZING or **RELAXING** bath salts, depending on the driver's mood; a shower; a toilet; a sink; and a toothbrush that dispensed Swiss cheese-flavored toothpaste!

The backseat could transform itself into a mini-kitchen with an **OVEN** and a small **STORAGE** area stocked with all the finest cheeses. And the front seat could become a tiny office with a **BUILT-IN LIBRARY** and a mini-desk for sudden brainstorms! For a writer like me, it was the **CAT'S MEOW**.

I had just finished reading the **ten-foot-tall** manual when Rusty and Professor von Volt came in.

"Did you finish giving Sol the once-over?" I asked him.

"Not yet," Rusty replied with a **shake** of his head. "There's still one **LITTLE** thing

I need to do, and then Sol will be ready. But how about you? Are you **ready**? Did you study for the driver's test? And did you read the **ENORMOUSE** manual? Huh? Did you? **DID YOU?**"

My whiskers trembled with stress.

"I did my **BEST**!" I squeaked nervously. "I think I understand it all, except for one thing: How does Sol **DISAPPEAR**?"

"It's simple," Professor von Volt answered. "Sol emits a special *reflective* screen that **mirrors** its surroundings and **camouflages** it."

"**Incredible!**" I exclaimed. "Does the **SILVER** car disappear, too?"

"No," Rusty answered. "The silver car cannot **disappear**. That car is named *Lunar*. My sister, **CARLOTTA**, created it. She is the best electrical engineer on

Mouse Island, and she was part of the team that designed Solar."

He pulled a **picture** out of his wallet and showed it to me.

"This is Carlotta," he said with a sad **sigh**. "One day she suggested I use Solar to commit crimes like ROBBING BANKS.

Obviously, I refused. Then she tried to **STEAL** Sol! But Sol understood what was happening and was able to activate all its SAFETY mechanisms and **ANTITHEFT** devices.

"When we designed Sol, we equipped it with a code of ethics that would never allow it to do anything DISHONEST!" Professor von Volt added.

"Unfortunately, Carlotta stole the design and built another car similar to Sol, but without the **code of ethics!**" Rusty continued. "She even tried to **destroy** Sol, but she foiled her own plans by activating the **ALARM** system!"

"Carlotta fled with the stolen plans, but she lost one piece of them: the **sheet** with the instructions to render the car **invisible**!" Professor von Volt explained. "That's why **Lunar**, the car Carlotta built, can't disappear! And that's why she's constantly trying to capture **Solar**: She wants to discover the secret of its **INVISIBILITY** and then **DESTROY** it!"

MISSION IMPOSSIBLE!

I was shocked at what I had just heard. It was so **SAD** to hear that Carlotta wanted to use Solar's incredible **technological** advances to commit crimes. What an **unhappy** rodent Carlotta must be!

Rusty's voice **shook** me from my thoughts.

"Enough moping!" Rusty squeaked. "You're about to go on your first **MISSION** as Solar's driver. But before you can **drive** Solar, you have to pass the driving **TEST**. Are you **READY**? **Let's go!**"

My whiskers trembled with excitement and **FEAR**. Rusty handed me the test.

To pass the *written* part of the exam, I had to:

1. Answer all ten questions.
2. Not make a single mistake!

For the driving part of the **exam**, I had to drive Sol around for **twenty** minutes while Rusty and Professor von Volt watched from a **hidden** camera.

"If you make even the **tiniest** mistake, we'll see it **IMMEDIATELY**!" Rusty told me. "If you drive **well**, we'll renew your license. But if you drive **poorly**, Sol will **fling** you out of the car, and we won't renew your license!"

"Yikes!" I squeaked *nervously*. "I'll try my **best**!"

I started the written part of the test. *Incredibly*, I managed to answer all ten questions without making even the *teensiest* error!

"Well done, Geronimo!" Rusty said with

a **GRiN**. "Now comes the fun part: the **DRIVING** test! Are you **REEEEADY**?"

At that moment, **Sol** came toward me slowly. Next to it was **MARGO BITMOUSE**. Her big green eyes made my **heart** skip a beat!

Sol **revved** its motor.

"*WHAT IS THE HOLDUP, STILTON?*" Sol asked. "*ARE YOU GETTING IN OR NOT?*"

Margo Bitmouse squeezed my shoulder and **smiled** at me.

Good luck, Geronimo!

"Now it's up to you, Geronimo!" she said. "Do your best!"

"Make sure you **pass**!" Rusty ordered me. "Don't make me look bad."

"Take care of Sol," Professor von Volt said **nervously**. "It's the only **prototype** of its kind in the **world**!"

I placed my paw on my HEART.

"I promise to defend Sol with my **LIFE**," I said solemnly. "I give you my word. RODENT'S HONOR!"

"We have to ask you to never divulge the location of our secret LABORATORY," Margo Bitmouse added.

"I will never **REVEAL** it to anyone," I promised. "I give you my word. RODENT'S HONOR!"

"Then it's time for you to begin your first **mission**," Margo Bitmouse said.

"And your DRIVING TEST!" Rusty added.

"Um, what **exactly** does this mission entail?" I asked with a squeak.

"Find **Lunar**, retrieve Duchess Catherine Rodenton's seventy-three-carat diamond necklace, and return it to New Mouse City's Mouseum."

"*W-what?*" I asked.

"B-but I can't do all that! It's **impossible**! I have to **drive** in the mayor's ceremony tomorrow!"

"*WELL, THEN WE WILL HAVE TO FINISH THIS MISSION IN ONE NIGHT,*" Solar said calmly.

Professor von Volt handed me a pair of GOLDEN MIRRORED glasses.

"When you wear these, you and Sol will be able to **COMMUNICATE** more easily," he told me.

I opened Sol's door and climbed in.

"Good luck, Stilton!" Rusty said. "Do

your best on the **DRIVING TEST**! Don't make me look bad!"

I put on the GOLDEN glasses and was instantly connected directly with Sol's circuits. It was as if our brains were one! **Incredible!**

The elevator took us **up, up, up,** and we found ourselves on the street. I checked to make sure no one had seen us, and then I drove down a side street.

"*THANK YOU FOR SAYING YOU WOULD DEFEND ME WITH YOUR LIFE,*" Solar said. "*I WOULD DO THE SAME FOR YOU.*"

"Thank you," I replied, moved by the gesture.

"*YOU ARE WELCOME,*" Solar said. "*NOW, LET US GET DOWN TO BUSINESS. IT IS THE PERFECT NIGHT TO LOOK FOR LUNAR. LUNAR IS MORE ACTIVE AT NIGHT BECAUSE IT USES MOONBEAMS TO RECHARGE.*"

Sol connected its computer to a **satellite** orbiting New Mouse City. Photos taken by the satellite appeared **INSTANTLY** on the computer's screen. Solar began scanning one photo after another at an **INCREDIBLE** speed until one of the photos showed a silver SILHOUETTE.

It was *Lunar*! And it was at New Mouse

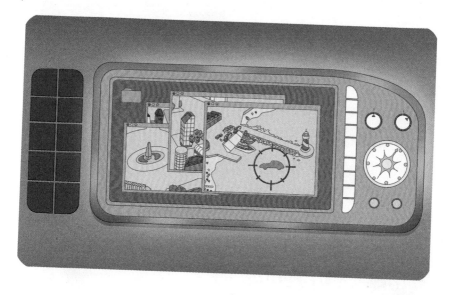

City's port. I drove **Sol** toward the docks, all the while being very careful to **SiGNaL** according to the rules of the road. (After all, I was taking a **TEST**!)

Solar and I searched along the deserted piers all **NIGHT**. As *dawn* approached, we headed toward the **BEACH**. Suddenly, Sol came to a dead stop in front of what looked like the **TRACKS** of a car that had suddenly applied its *brakes*.

"LOOK!" Sol told me. *"THOSE TRACKS BELONG TO LUNAR!"*

I got out and looked around, confused. The **TRACKS** didn't seem to lead anywhere.

"Huh?" I asked. "Where did Lunar go?"

Sol activated its built-in **echo sounder** and began probing the bottom of the **sea**.

"I FOUND IT!" Sol said. *"LUNAR IS ON THE OCEAN FLOOR!"*

I saw a **LIGHT** at the bottom of the sea, and the water began to **bubble**.

Suddenly, Lunar rose to the surface like an enormouse silvery fish!

CARLOTTA CARR

The silvery car sat on the sand, DRIPPING with water. The driver's door opened, and a tall, thin rodent emerged.

It was **CARLOTTA CARR**!

She had long blonde fur and she was wearing a black outfit. She wore a necklace dripping with **diamonds** the size of **PLUMS**. It was Duchess Rodenton's **STOLEN** heirloom!

Carlotta Carr removed her silver mirrored sunglasses, and I saw her icy, **ruthless** eyes.

Suddenly, Rusty was standing by my side.

"First of all, **CONGRATS**!" he whispered in my ear. "You

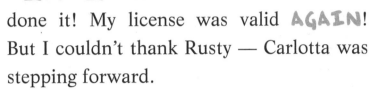

PASSED the test!"

Then he handed me my **DRiVeR'S LiCeNSe**. I had done it! My license was valid **AGAIN**! But I couldn't thank Rusty — Carlotta was stepping forward.

"Rusty, you finally found me," Carlotta **HISSED** maliciously. Then she cackled. "You and Solar were **very, very** slow!"

Rusty's eyes filled with **tears**.

"Oh, Carlotta, how you've changed!" he said **sadly**. "Your **heart** is so **cold**. Your ambition has **corrupted** you!"

Carlotta **laughed** at her brother.

"And you've stayed **exactly** the same, Rusty," she sneered. "You're still a **fool**."

She touched the **DIAMOND** necklace around her neck.

"Thanks to Lunar, look what I've got!" she

89

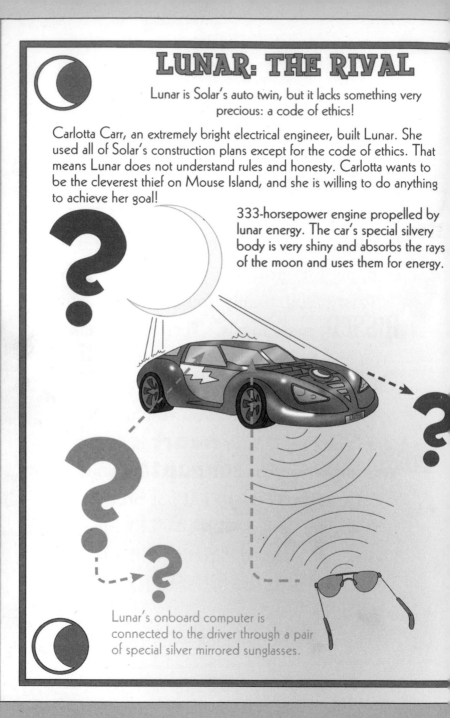

LUNAR: THE RIVAL

Lunar is Solar's auto twin, but it lacks something very precious: a code of ethics!

Carlotta Carr, an extremely bright electrical engineer, built Lunar. She used all of Solar's construction plans except for the code of ethics. That means Lunar does not understand rules and honesty. Carlotta wants to be the cleverest thief on Mouse Island, and she is willing to do anything to achieve her goal!

333-horsepower engine propelled by lunar energy. The car's special silvery body is very shiny and absorbs the rays of the moon and uses them for energy.

Lunar's onboard computer is connected to the driver through a pair of special silver mirrored sunglasses.

Lunar cannot instantly disappear because Carlotta couldn't re-create the electromagnetic screen that makes Solar invisible. The sheet with all the instructions was lost forever!

Lunar's massive silver medallion is shaped like the moon and measures the distance to all possible obstacles.

All of Lunar's metal parts are made of solid silver!

But are all of Lunar's accessories and gadgets the same as Solar's? No one but Carlotta knows the answer to that question!

said. "And this is just the beginning! I have lots of plans for the FUTURE."

"Give me the necklace!" Rusty ordered.

But Carlotta just laughed.

"I have no intention of doing that," she said. "But I will agree to a duel between these cars. If Solar wins, you take the necklace. And if I win, I take Solar."

Rusty and I were about to refuse when Solar spoke.

Carlotta...

"I ACCEPT THE CHALLENGE."

The two vehicles turned to face each other, and the duel began.

First the two cars tried to **melt** the other's circuits with huge electrical charges. But both of their *computers* were shielded and impossible to break through.

Then Lunar activated a very powerful *magnet*. The magnet **attracted** all metal objects in the area to Lunar's body.

Rusty . . .

The keys and coins I had in my pocket **flew** toward the silver car's **magnet**. Even my *belt buckle* was drawn to the magnet. *Squeak!*

But Solar came to my **RESCUE**. It activated an **ANTIMAGNETIC** device and unleashed its **secret** weapon: a cloud of robot **mosquitoes** that attacked Lunar!

Carlotta took one look at the robot mosquitoes and **gave up**.

"Enough!" she snarled **nastily**. "You **WON**! But this is not the end."

She **ripped** the diamond necklace off her neck and threw it in the water.

"If you want the necklace, go get it!" she **shrieked**. "But you'll never have me!"

She jumped inside Lunar, **revved**

up the engine, and drove off in a cloud of SMOKE.

I was **torn**. Should I go after Carlotta or try to **save** the necklace?

"Quick! Let's get the *necklace*!" I said.

Sol **DOVE** into the water. A long arm holding a net extended from the passenger-side door and scooped up the necklace before the sea could **swallow** it.

When Sol emerged from the water, I realized that the **sun** was high on the HORIZON. I checked the time.

"**Crusty cat litter!**" I squeaked **hysterically**. "I'm going to be late for the mayor's ceremony! I have to be at City Hall in fifteen minutes!"

An Extremely Difficult Course

Solar figured out the shortest route to City Hall, and Rusty got in the driver's seat. He maneuvered so well in **TRAFFIC** that we arrived right as the clock struck eight thirty. Solar parked down the block and waited for my signal.

The mayor was already at the podium, about to begin the **CEREMONY**, and I saw my grandfather William Shortpaws and my entire FAMILY nearby. The crowd was also full of reporters and TV news crews for all the *national* and international stations.

"And now, Mr. Geronimo Stilton will give us a **DEMONSTRATION** on how to drive safely!" the mayor announced. "Which car will you use for the **DEMONSTRATION**?"

I snapped my fingers, and Solar appeared.

"**OOOOOOOH!**" the crowd shouted.

When Sol pulled up, the photographers began **SNAPPING** one photo after another, and the reporters fired all sorts of questions at me.

"Mr. Stilton, how does it **feel** to drive this type of car?"

"Who designed it?"

"It's a great honor to drive **Solar**!" I replied with a smile. "As far as who designed it, I'm sorry but I can't tell you that. It's a **SECRET**!" I climbed into the car and turned on the *ignition*.

"Are you ready, Sol?" I whispered.

Sol revved its engine in reply.

"*I WILL NOT HELP YOU WITH THE DEMONSTRATION*," Sol said. "*YOU HAVE TO DO IT ALL BY YOURSELF!*"

It was an **extremely difficult** obstacle course. Sol was perfectly silent the entire time. It didn't give me any tips, it didn't **DRIVE** for me, and it didn't help me through

any of the more DIFFICULT parts. My whiskers trembled the entire time!

To stay calm, I reminded myself that, thanks to my friend Rusty Carr, I had my license again. I could do this! I just had to stay calm and relaxed! I concentrated on all I had LEARNED in the last week.

When I got to the end of the course, I got out of the car.

"H-how did I do?" I asked Sol.

"YOU WERE PERFECT," Sol said.

"Congratulations!" the mayor agreed. "You didn't make a SINGLE mistake!"

He asked me to join him onstage, where he shook my paw. I saw Rusty in the crowd, and I called him onto the stage as well.

"Thank you, dear friend," I said. "Without your driving lessons, I never could have done it!"

Rusty was PLEASED with the compliment, but he was also very modest.

"It was all your doing, Geronimo," Rusty said to me. "Your driving was SUPERB!"

Then he turned to address the crowd.

"I am happy to announce that *Geronimo Stilton* and this amazing car have recovered Duchess Catherine Rodenton's diamond necklace!"

Congratulations!

YOU HELPED ME,
NOW I'LL HELP YOU!

The photographers began snapping one photo after another while Rusty and I gave the stolen *necklace* to the mayor to return to the duchess.

Then suddenly, Rusty rushed off the stage.

"Sorry, I have to run!" he **squeaked**

anxiously. "I have to finish **PAINTING** the driving school headquarters. All the work has to be done to*day*!"

"Well, I'm coming with you!" I told him with a SMILE. "You helped me, and now I'll help you. In fact, I'll ask my entire **family** to help as well!"

I got my sister, Thea, my cousin Trap, my nephew Benjamin, and a lot of other FRieNDS, including Bruce Hyena, Petunia

Pretty Paws, Bugsy Wugsy, Wild Willie, and Hercule Poirat to HELP out. **Rusty's** relatives pitched in, too: Professor von Volt, Dewey von Volt, Margo Bitmouse, and Rob-8 were **all** there!

We all worked together HAPPiLY, and the following day, the freshly painted headquarters of The Very Best Driving School in New Mouse City looked perfect!

And so, my rodent friends, that is the end of my latest *ADVENTURE*.

Oh, and I almost forgot: Whether you travel by FooT, on a bicycle, or in a *car*, always RESPECT the rules of the road.

See you next time, and until then, stay safe on your city's streets!

GERONIMO'S 10 RULES OF THE ROAD

1. Obey all traffic signs.
2. Always cross the street in the crosswalk.
3. Always wait for a walk signal before you cross the street.
4. Always look to the right and to the left before you cross the street.
5. Always walk on the sidewalk.
6. If there is no sidewalk, walk close to the curb on the left hand side of the road facing oncoming traffic.
7. When riding a bike, always wear a helmet.
8. When riding a bike, keep to the right and don't ride on the sidewalk.
9. Take care of your bicycle. Your brakes, tires, chain, lights, and bell must be in good working condition.
10. Be sure to buckle your seat belt when riding in a car (or in any moving vehicle).

Stay safe!

See you next time!

Don't miss any of my other fabumouse adventures!

#1 Lost Treasure of the Emerald Eye

#2 The Curse of the Cheese Pyramid

#3 Cat and Mouse in a Haunted House

#4 I'm Too Fond of My Fur!

#5 Four Mice Deep in the Jungle

#6 Paws Off, Cheddarface!

#7 Red Pizzas for a Blue Count

#8 Attack of the Bandit Cats

#9 A Fabumouse Vacation for Geronimo

#10 All Because of a Cup of Coffee

#11 It's Halloween, You 'Fraidy Mouse!

#12 Merry Christmas, Geronimo!

#13 The Phantom of the Subway

#14 The Temple of the Ruby of Fire

#15 The Mona Mousa Code

#16 A Cheese-Colored Camper

#17 Watch Your Whiskers, Stilton!

#18 Shipwreck on the Pirate Islands

#19 My Name Is Stilton, Geronimo Stilton

#20 Surf's Up, Geronimo!

#21 The Wild, Wild West

#22 The Secret of Cacklefur Castle

A Christmas Tale

#23 Valentine's Day Disaster

#24 Field Trip to Niagara Falls

#25 The Search for Sunken Treasure

#26 The Mummy with No Name

#27 The Christmas Toy Factory

#28 Wedding Crasher

#29 Down and Out Down Under

#30 The Mouse Island Marathon

#31 The Mysterious Cheese Thief

Christmas Catastrophe

#32 Valley of the Giant Skeletons

#33 Geronimo and the Gold Medal Mystery

#34 Geronimo Stilton, Secret Agent

#35 A Very Merry Christmas

#36 Geronimo's Valentine

#37 The Race Across America

#38 A Fabumouse School Adventure

#39 Singing Sensation

#40 The Karate Mouse

#41 Mighty Mount Kilimanjaro

#42 The Peculiar Pumpkin Thief

#43 I'm Not a Supermouse!

#44 The Giant Diamond Robbery

#45 Save the White Whale!

#46 The Haunted Castle

#47 Run for the Hills, Geronimo!

#48 The Mystery in Venice

#49 The Way of the Samurai

#50 This Hotel Is Haunted

#51 The Enormouse Pearl Heist

#52 Mouse in Space!

#53 Rumble in the Jungle

#54 Get into Gear, Stilton!

Up next!

#55 The Golden Statue Plot

Check out these exciting *Thea Sisters* adventures!

Thea Stilton and the Dragon's Code

Thea Stilton and the Mountain of Fire

Thea Stilton and the Ghost of the Shipwreck

Thea Stilton and the Secret City

Thea Stilton and the Mystery in Paris

Thea Stilton and the Cherry Blossom Adventure

Thea Stilton and the Star Castaways

Thea Stilton: Big Trouble in the Big Apple

Thea Stilton and the Ice Treasure

Thea Stilton and the Secret of the Old Castle

Thea Stilton and the Blue Scarab Hunt

Thea Stilton and the Prince's Emerald

Thea Stilton and the Mystery on the Orient Express

Thea Stilton and the Dancing Shadows

Thea Stilton and the Legend of the Fire Flowers

Thea Stilton and the Spanish Dance Mission

Thea Stilton and the Journey to the Lion's Den

Be sure
to read all
my adventures
in the Kingdom
of Fantasy!

**THE KINGDOM
OF FANTASY**

**THE QUEST FOR
PARADISE:**
THE RETURN TO THE
KINGDOM OF FANTASY

**THE AMAZING
VOYAGE:**
THE THIRD ADVENTURE
IN THE KINGDOM
OF FANTASY

**THE DRAGON
PROPHECY:**
THE FOURTH ADVENTURE
IN THE KINGDOM
OF FANTASY

**THE VOLCANO
OF FIRE:**
THE FIFTH ADVENTURE
IN THE KINGDOM
OF FANTASY

Check out these very special editions featuring me and the Thea Sisters!

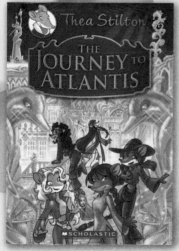

THE JOURNEY TO ATLANTIS

THE SECRET OF THE FAIRIES

Meet
CREEPELLA VON CACKLEFUR

I, *Geronimo Stilton*, have a lot of mouse friends, but none as **spooky** as my friend CREEPELLA VON CACKLEFUR! She is an enchanting and MYSTERIOUS mouse with a pet bat named Bitewing. YIKES! I'm a real 'fraidy mouse, but even I think CREEPELLA and her family are AWFULLY fascinating. I can't wait for you to read all about CREEPELLA in these fa-mouse-ly funny and **spectacularly spooky** tales!

#1 THE THIRTEEN GHOSTS

#2 MEET ME IN HORRORWOOD

#3 GHOST PIRATE TREASURE

#4 RETURN OF THE VAMPIRE

#5 FRIGHT NIGHT

Meet
GERONIMO STILTONOOT

He is a cavemouse — Geronimo Stilton's ancient ancestor! He runs the stone newspaper in the prehistoric village of Old Mouse City. From dealing with dinosaurs to dodging meteorites, his life in the Stone Age is full of adventure!

ABOUT THE AUTHOR

Born in New Mouse City, Mouse Island, **GERONIMO STILTON** is Rattus Emeritus of Mousomorphic Literature and of Neo-Ratonic Comparative Philosophy. For the past twenty years, he has been running *The Rodent's Gazette*, New Mouse City's most widely read daily newspaper.

Stilton was awarded the Ratitzer Prize for his scoops on *The Curse of the Cheese Pyramid* and *The Search for Sunken Treasure*. He has also received the Andersen 2000 Prize for Personality of the Year. One of his bestsellers won the 2002 eBook Award for world's best ratlings' electronic book. His works have been published all over the globe.

In his spare time, Mr. Stilton collects antique cheese rinds and plays golf. But what he most enjoys is telling stories to his nephew Benjamin.

1. Main entrance
2. Printing presses (where the books and newspaper are printed)
3. Accounts department
4. Editorial room (where the editors, illustrators, and designers work)
5. Geronimo Stilton's office
6. Helicopter landing pad

THE RODENT'S GAZETTE

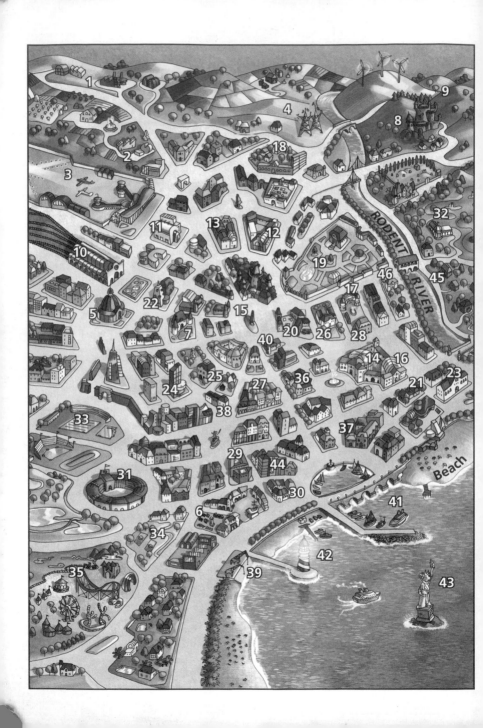

Map of New Mouse City

1. Industrial Zone
2. Cheese Factories
3. Angorat International Airport
4. WRAT Radio and Television Station
5. Cheese Market
6. Fish Market
7. Town Hall
8. Snotnose Castle
9. The Seven Hills of Mouse Island
10. Mouse Central Station
11. Trade Center
12. Movie Theater
13. Gym
14. Catnegie Hall
15. Singing Stone Plaza
16. The Gouda Theater
17. Grand Hotel
18. Mouse General Hospital
19. Botanical Gardens
20. Cheap Junk for Less (Trap's store)
21. Aunt Sweetfur and Benjamin's House
22. Museum of Modern Art
23. University and Library
24. *The Daily Rat*
25. *The Rodent's Gazette*
26. Trap's House
27. Fashion District
28. The Mouse House Restaurant
29. Environmental Protection Center
30. Harbor Office
31. Mousidon Square Garden
32. Golf Course
33. Swimming Pool
34. Tennis Courts
35. Curlyfur Island Amusement Park
36. Geronimo's House
37. Historic District
38. Public Library
39. Shipyard
40. Thea's House
41. New Mouse Harbor
42. Luna Lighthouse
43. The Statue of Liberty
44. Hercule Poirat's Office
45. Petunia Pretty Paws's House
46. Grandfather William's House

Map of Mouse Island

1. Big Ice Lake
2. Frozen Fur Peak
3. Slipperyslopes Glacier
4. Coldcreeps Peak
5. Ratzikistan
6. Transratania
7. Mount Vamp
8. Roastedrat Volcano
9. Brimstone Lake
10. Poopedcat Pass
11. Stinko Peak
12. Dark Forest
13. Vain Vampires Valley
14. Goose Bumps Gorge
15. The Shadow Line Pass
16. Penny Pincher Castle
17. Nature Reserve Park
18. Las Ratayas Marinas
19. Fossil Forest
20. Lake Lake
21. Lake Lakelake
22. Lake Lakelakelake
23. Cheddar Crag
24. Cannycat Castle
25. Valley of the Giant Sequoia
26. Cheddar Springs
27. Sulfurous Swamp
28. Old Reliable Geyser
29. Vole Vale
30. Ravingrat Ravine
31. Gnat Marshes
32. Munster Highlands
33. Mousehara Desert
34. Oasis of the Sweaty Camel
35. Cabbagehead Hill
36. Rattytrap Jungle
37. Rio Mosquito

Dear mouse friends,
Thanks for reading, and farewell
till the next book.
It'll be another whisker-licking-good
adventure, and that's a promise!

Geronimo Stilton